SCOOTER
The Mischievous Elf

By
James B. Dworkin

Illustrated by
Mike Jenneman

ISBN: 9781693636042

This book is dedicated to my two youngest grandchildren, Henry and Theo. One night they asked me to make up a Christmas story and this is the story that evolved from that very special evening.

James B. Dworkin

As usual, Santa's workshop was bustling with toy making activity. But...

1

COUNTDOWN TO CHRISTMAS

MONTHS	WEEKS	DAYS	HOURS	MINUTES	SECONDS
04	03	04	09	21	13

PAPER & RIBBON

SANTA'S LETTERS

TO DO LIST
- Restock Toy Parts
- Sort Santa's Letters & en
- Paint Toy Parts
- Organize Finished Toys
- Feed Reindeer
- Clean Reindeer Stable
- Polish Santa's Sleigh
- Shovel the Sidewalks
- FAA Airport Approvals
- Upgrade EPS!

CHLOE

ZIPPY

BEEZLE

?

RUDY

Santa Claus needed to hire one more elf to help him finish the Christmas toys and gifts.

2

Santa liked to know each elf,
so he spoke to many potential helpers
who wanted the job. But the one elf he
decided to hire as his newest helper was...

SCOOTER!

Scooter seemed like he would be a good elf, but Santa was unaware that this elf had a devious plan.

For each night after he was done making toys, he would sneak under Santa's sleigh and do something very conniving.

Scooter was slowly and meticulously making a secret zipper on the bottom of the gigantic toy bag Santa used to bring Christmas presents to all the good little girls and boys.

Scooter was also making a secret trap door under Santa's sleigh so he could enter into the bottom of the the toy bag through the sleigh.

It took him many nights to finish the zipper and the trap door. When it was done, he also made a secret hiding pouch for himself at the bottom of Santa's bag.

On Christmas Eve, as Santa prepared to go on his journey, Scooter was hidden in Santa's sleigh. What was Scooter going to do? Why was he hiding in Santa's sleigh??

It turns out that Scooter was from a place called Pixie Island, which was undetectable because it was almost always covered by clouds. His home town was Vander Village. Scooter knew Santa's sleigh would be flying right over his island shortly after taking off from the North Pole.

Chandrella

Tuckerville

Warloc Woods

Vander Village

Misty Mountai

PIXIE
ISLAND

Partridge Point

Lexicon

Stanley Clark School

Brooks School Bears

BROOKS SCHOOL BEARS

Westermere

Zandro

St. John Church

Dragon's Cove

Geisville

At just the moment when the reindeer were flying Santa's sleigh over the island, Scooter unzipped the bottom of Santa's bag. He jumped out and rode down on a toy parachute.

12

The sky over Pixie Island was filled with falling toys which Scooter distributed to all of the good little girls and boys.

All of the children on Pixie Island were surprised and happy to have such a wonderful Christmas with so many toys... But what happened with Santa Claus and the rest of the children around the world?

Santa sensed that something was wrong as the reindeer were pulling his sleigh so much faster than usual.

16

His first stop of the night was at the house of little boys Henry and Theo and their sister Kate. As Santa went to open his bag, he saw that it was completely empty! Where were all of the presents?

Santa also saw an open zipper at the bottom of his bag with a letter "S," only worn by one elf -- Scooter. Santa knew who took the toys, but first he had to deliver toys to all the other good children.

Even though his bag was empty, Santa had a lot of magic that he could perform. Putting his finger on the side of his nose, he recited this magic phrase...

"Jingle, Jangle Make Some NOISE For All The Good Little Girls and Boys. Fill My Bag With Christmas Toys!"

Just like that, the zipper disappeared and his bag was full once again. Santa was easily able to finish delivering all the presents that night.

Usually, after delivering the last present, Santa was so tired that he went straight back to the North Pole and took a long nap. But not this night. He had one more very important stop to make.

Scooter's House

PIXIE ISLAND

Santa told his reindeer to find Scooter using EPS (Elf Positioning System). The reindeer took Santa right to Scooter's house on Pixie Island, where Scooter was cozily tucked in his bed. Santa could not remember ever being to Pixie Island before. Maybe it was because he was so tired?

LAST HOUSE

Tuckerville

Scooter's House

Vander Village

PIXIE
ISLAND

Needless to say, Scooter was shocked when he woke up to see
Santa Claus towering over him at his bedside. Scooter didn't
know what to say or do. But Santa spoke first and handed
Scooter a letter to read...

Scooter told Santa he was sorry for what he had done. He hoped Santa wouldn't be mad at him. He also told Santa he didn't deserve any presents this year because of what he had done. But he wanted to explain to Santa why he had done it.

But before Scooter could explain, Santa told him how he
had admired his excellent work during the past year.
He was undecided about what to do with Scooter.

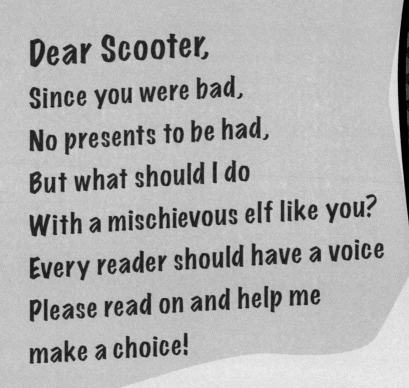

Dear Scooter,
Since you were bad,
No presents to be had,
But what should I do
With a mischievous elf like you?
Every reader should have a voice
Please read on and help me
make a choice!

Santa

WHAT SHOULD SANTA DO?

Santa needed to teach the mischievous Scooter a lesson. He decided to keep a close eye on him by assigning Scooter to the very end of the toy making line. He will be counting thousands of gumballs each day. Scooter will not be a leader or be able to use his imagination or creativity until he can be a good elf once again.

PAPER & RIBBON

SANTA'S LETTERS

TO DO LIST

- Restock Toy Parts
- Sort Santa's Letters & email
- Count ALL gumballs
- Organize Finished Toys
- Feed Reindeer
- Clean Reindeer Stable
- Polish Santa's Sleigh
- Shovel the Sidewalks
- FAA Airport Approvals
- Upgrade EPS!

CHLOE

ZIPPY

BEEZLE

RUDY

2

Santa was so disappointed and upset with Scooter that he ended up giving his position in the toy making line to a good elf. Scooter was sent back to Pixie Island to never work for Santa again.

PIXIE ISLAND

Tuckerville

Scooter's House

Vander Village

OR...

Santa needed to teach Scooter a lesson. He decided to make him the Reindeer Stable Elf for the whole year. Santa thought that if Scooter had to scoop up reindeer poop each day, he would never be mischievous again!

OR...

Santa decided to send Scooter to the **FRIGID COLD**, boring, lonely and unfriendly **SOUTH POLE** to make him realize how good he had it at the North Pole. Only penguins, seals, birds, and killer whales live there.

Scooter trying to survive in the South Pole

1

Santa sends Scooter to the very end of the toy making line to count gumballs.

2

Santa decides to fire Scooter and not use him as an elf anymore.

PIXIE ISLAND

Tuckerville

Scooter's House

Vander Village

3

Santa makes Scooter the Reindeer Stable Elf.

4

Santa sends Scooter to the South Pole.

Scooter trying to survive the South Pole

Before Santa could make up his mind about Scooter's punishment, the elf had the chance to explain why he had pulled off this Christmas Eve trickery.

As it turns out, Scooter explained to Santa that the kids on Pixie Island had been accidentally overlooked by Santa Claus for many years, as the Island was hardly visible through the thick fog and clouds. Scooter's plan had been to make sure that the children on Pixie Island finally would receive some presents.

When Santa learned of the absolute good intention behind Scooter's plan, he thanked him and... Santa agreed that from now on each Christmas Eve, his very first stop would be at Pixie Island.

Thanks to the elf
by the name of:

S

SCOOTER!

Made in the
USA
Middletown, DE